PRACTICE MAKES PERFECT

by Polly Peterson • illustrated by Matt Straub

Harcourt

Orlando   Boston   Dallas   Chicago   San Diego

Visit *The Learning Site!*

www.harcourtschool.com

School is not the only place to learn. You can learn a lot of things when you are not at school, too. Do you have any special interests? Do you have a favorite activity? Let's meet some children who do.

Ramon loved kicking a soccer ball even when he was very little. When he was in first grade, he joined a soccer team. The coach taught the team a lot of practice drills. He taught them the rules of the game.

By the time Ramon was in third grade,
he was playing soccer almost every day.
He played soccer with his friends at recess.
He played soccer after school.

Ramon and his friends practice their drills even when the coach is not there. Ramon scored a goal in yesterday's game. His coach says that he is becoming a really strong player.

Luis is Ramon's brother. He likes playing soccer, too, but he doesn't play on a team. He is too busy playing music.

Luis plays the piano. The kind of music he wants to play is not easy to learn. He practices every day. He knows that he will be able to play well if he tries hard.

Jenny goes to art classes every week. She likes working with clay. Her first pots were not very good. Each pot she makes is a little better than the last. Today she made a beautiful vase.

When Samantha first went to the swimming pool, she was afraid to put her face in the water. Learning how to swim was hard. It took a whole summer of practice. Now she loves the water. She is learning how to dive.

Cynthia, Sam, and Maria go to an acting class after school. They are learning how to put on a play. Their first play was the folktale called "Cinderella."

First, they memorized their lines. Then, they practiced a lot. They learned where to stand. They learned how to speak so that everyone could hear them. At last, they were ready for the performance. It was a lot of work, but it was worth it!

Tim and Felicia both love to play the game of baseball. Baseball is hard to practice alone. So Tim and Felicia meet at a park every Saturday. They throw and catch the ball. They practice batting and pitching.

Kenji got in-line skates for his birthday. When he put them on, he couldn't go anywhere. He kept falling down. He fell again and again, but he didn't give up. Now he can skate everywhere without falling.

Emilio loves to draw. He draws on paper. He draws with chalk on the sidewalk. His parents even let him draw a mural on their basement wall! Now Emilio is learning how to draw cartoons. He hopes to be a cartoonist some day.

Yolanda plays the violin. Her friend Rachel plays the flute. They are learning some music to play together. They practice every day. Next month they will play together in a school show.

What do all these children have in
common? They don't all like the same
activities. They do all agree on one thing.
Doing something well is hard work. It takes
practice, practice, and more practice!